REVENGE OF THE PHANTOM FURBALL

For Alice and Archie – SH

For Joe, number one cool cat – SC

STRIPES PUBLISHING
An imprint of the Little Tiger Group
1 The Coda Centre, 189 Munster Road, London SW6 6AW

Imported into the EEA by Penguin Random House Ireland, Morrison
Chambers, 32 Nassau Street, Dublin D02 YH68

A paperback original
First published in Great Britain in 2012

Text copyright © Sam Hay, 2012
Illustrations copyright © Simon Cooper, 2012

ISBN: 978-1-84715-289-3

The right of Sam Hay and Simon Cooper to be identified as the author and illus-
trator of this work respectively has been asserted by them in accordance with the
Copyright, Designs and Patents Act, 1988.

All rights reserved.

A CIP catalogue record for this book is available from the British Library.

This book is sold subject to the condition that it shall not, by
way of trade or otherwise, be lent, resold, hired out, or otherwise circulated
without the publisher's prior consent in any form of binding or cover other than
that in which it is published and without a similar condition, including this
condition, being imposed upon the subsequent purchaser.

Printed and bound in China.

MIX
Paper from
responsible sources
FSC® C169965

The Forest Stewardship Council® (FSC®) is a global, not-for-profit
organization dedicated to the promotion of responsible forest
management worldwide. FSC defines standards based on agreed
principles for responsible forest stewardship that
are supported by environmental, social, and
economic stakeholders.
To learn more, visit www.fsc.org

STP/2700/0469/0622

10 9 8 7 6 5 4 3

UNDEAD PETS

REVENGE OF THE PHANTOM FURBALL

SAM HAY
ILLUSTRATED BY SIMON COOPER

LITTLE TIGER
LONDON

The story so far...

Ten-year-old Joe Edmunds is desperate for a pet.

But his mum's allergies mean that he's got no chance.

Then his great-uncle Charlie gives him an ancient Egyptian amulet that he claims will grant Joe a single wish...

But instead of getting a pet, Joe becomes the Protector of Undead Pets. He is bound by the amulet to solve the problems of zombie pets so they can pass peacefully to the afterlife.

And so the trouble begins...

CHAPTER ONE

It was Saturday morning, and Joe was in the paint department of the local DIY superstore. He was just wondering what colour he could make if he blended orange, purple and gold paint, when, out of the corner of his eye, he saw a streak of grey disappearing under the shelves.

"What was that?" he said.

"Mmm?" muttered Dad, who was reading the labels on the paint tins. He didn't look up.

Joe's big sister, Sarah, frowned. "I didn't see anything."

UNDEAD PETS

"It was grey, sort of like a squirrel or something," said Joe, crouching down and peering under the shelves to see where it had gone.

Sarah rolled her eyes. "They don't let squirrels in shops, weirdo!"

Joe scowled and tried to think of a clever reply, but just then his little brother, Toby, whizzed past, doing a wheelie with the shopping trolley.

"Look out!" called Dad.

"Hey!" yelped Sarah, jumping out of the way.

Joe grinned. With a bit of luck Toby would get her next time! He turned back to the paint charts and was about to invent another crazy colour combination, when suddenly he saw it again – a flash of movement out of the corner of his eye. He turned sharply and saw a tail disappearing round the top of the aisle.

"There it is!" he yelled. "Look, Dad!"

"Hmm?" Dad looked up. "What is it, Joe?"

"A squirrel out doing its shopping, apparently," Sarah smirked.

"I definitely saw something," huffed Joe.

"OK, OK," said Dad, trying to soothe the situation. "Maybe it was a guide dog – they're allowed in shops."

Joe was about to explain that it was smaller than a guide dog, when Toby whizzed past again.

"Stop that!" Dad reached out and grabbed the trolley, stopping it dead. He sighed. "The sooner you let me concentrate on choosing this paint, the sooner we can get out of here." He turned to Sarah. "Hurry up and decide which colour you want for your bedroom. Toby, you hold the trolley still while I load it up. And Joe, can you go and find me a plug for the bath? Which reminds me, you still need to get a new sponge for your mum!"

UNDEAD PETS

Joe's face reddened. Mum's last bath sponge had been chewed up by an undead pet that visited him — a zombie hamster named Dumpling with a huge appetite! Not that his parents knew that. No one else had been able to see the hamster apart from Joe. So he'd got the blame for the mangled sponge — not to mention turning their kitchen upside down and scoffing his headteacher's packed lunch!

"And don't forget you promised to pay for it out of your pocket money," added Dad. "It'll be a nice surprise for Mum when she gets back from work."

Joe sighed. Sometimes life just wasn't fair!

The bathroom department was right at the back of the shop. Joe walked through the aisles, past towering shelves. There was an entire section filled with different loo seats. Joe had never

UNDEAD PETS

seen so many designs. There were all the usual ones, and some fancy ones, too – a shiny gold one, a see-through one with goldfish printed on it ... and a very weird one that looked like a shark's mouth. Joe smiled; he wished he could buy that to scare Sarah! He was just searching for bath plugs, when suddenly a small furry head popped out of one of the display toilets.

"Whoa!" Joe jumped. It definitely wasn't a guide dog, but it wasn't a squirrel either. It was a cat – an odd-looking silvery-grey cat that was covered in dirty bandages. As soon as it spotted Joe, it shot out of the toilet like a cannonball, straight into his arms, and gripped on tightly with its claws.

"Ow!" Joe yelped, as the cat clawed its way up to his shoulder where it perched like a parrot, peering into his face. Joe winced. Its breath smelled of rotten fish.

"You're Joe, aren't you?" it yowled in a high-pitched voice. "Joe Edmunds, the keeper of the Amulet of Anubis? I need your help!"

UNDEAD PETS

Joe groaned. Not another undead pet! It had been just over a week since Dumpling had visited, and things were just getting back to normal.

The cat nuzzled into his neck with its big furry face. Joe wrinkled his nose. Its breath really did pong.

"My name's Pickle," it said.

Joe rolled his eyes. "Don't tell me – you're in a bit of a pickle, Pickle!" But the cat didn't seem to find Joe's joke funny. She dug her claws deeper into his shoulder. "Hey! Stop that, it hurts!" Joe squeaked.

"I need your help to save my sister," whined the cat. "I've been trying to speak to you for days. But there's been so much horrible noise coming from your house that I've been too scared to get close. I hate noise!"

Joe frowned. What was the cat talking about? Then he remembered that Dad had been building Sarah a wardrobe using his power tools.

Pickle started to purr. "At least it's quiet here..."

Just then there was a loud PING-PONG from above them, and a booming voice echoed around the shop.

SHOP ASSISTANT TO THE LAWNMOWER DEPARTMENT! URGENT CUSTOMER ENQUIRY!

Pickle leaped out of Joe's arms with a howl and darted away.

"Hey," Joe called, "it's only the tannoy!" But Pickle wasn't listening. As she sped across the shop floor, Joe noticed that her bandages were beginning to unravel. "Watch out!" he called.

But it was too late. Pickle tripped over the trailing bandages, landing with a thump on the shiny lino and skidding wildly out of control. She finally came to a stop when she crashed head first into a pyramid of paint tins.

CHAPTER TWO

"Uh-oh," Joe muttered.

There were tins everywhere – rolling down the aisle, disappearing under the shelves – and right in the middle of the chaos was Pickle, doing her best to dodge them. As she jumped out of the way, she bumped into a display of windscreen washer fluid stacked into a great tower. The bottles wobbled, then slowly began to topple.

"Help!" yowled Pickle, leaping out of the way.

Undead Pets

Several of the bottles split as they hit the ground, spilling everywhere. Joe watched as a puddle oozed across the floor towards Pickle. "Look out!" he called.

Yowling and howling, Pickle took off once more, her paws sliding as she disappeared round the corner of the aisle. Joe turned to see three shop assistants and the store manager appear behind him.

UNDEAD PETS

Joe glanced at the mess, then at the shop staff who were glaring at him crossly.

He gulped. "I can explain..." But he didn't get the chance to try, because just then there was a loud CRASH! from the other side of the store, followed by the sound of breaking glass.

"That way!" shouted the store manager as he took off down the aisle, leaping over the lake of spilt liquid. His staff followed close behind, and Joe brought up the rear.

"It came from the lighting department," the store manager called, just as there was another CRASH!

Joe turned the corner and gasped. Hundreds of different lampshades were on display, and two large glass chandeliers lay shattered on the ground. Peering down from the metal beams high above them was an anxious-looking Pickle. Her fur was standing on end and her tail was swishing to and fro.

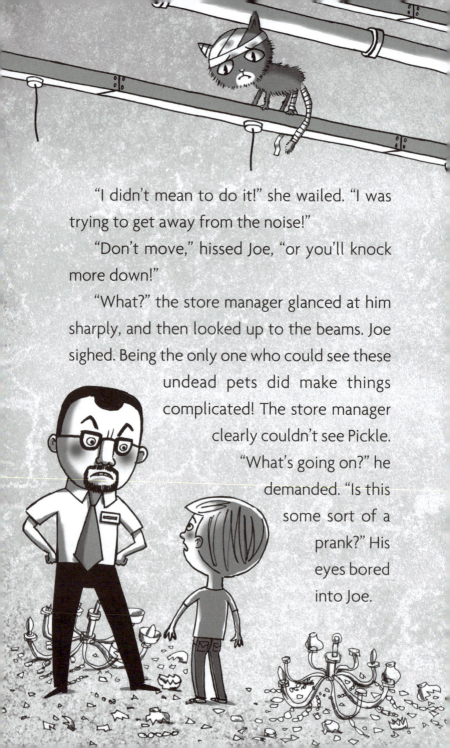

"I didn't mean to do it!" she wailed. "I was trying to get away from the noise!"

"Don't move," hissed Joe, "or you'll knock more down!"

"What?" the store manager glanced at him sharply, and then looked up to the beams. Joe sighed. Being the only one who could see these undead pets did make things complicated! The store manager clearly couldn't see Pickle.

"What's going on?" he demanded. "Is this some sort of a prank?" His eyes bored into Joe.

"No! Of course not!" Joe squeaked.

The store manager glared at him, then turned to his assistant. "Get this glass cleared up immediately, and put out an announcement that the lighting department is closed until further notice."

Joe gasped. Not another announcement! Pickle was sitting right next to the loudspeaker – she'd get the fright of her life! But there was no way he could warn her, as the store manager still had his beady eyes fixed on Joe.

"What's your name? Where are your parents?"

"My name's Joe, and … er … my dad's over there."

He pointed at Dad, who had just appeared with Sarah and Toby, pushing a trolley full of paint. Dad looked down at the mess, then at Joe standing in the middle of it. "What's going on?" he asked.

Joe was about to answer when suddenly the dreaded PING-PONG of a shop announcement blasted out above them.

"MEOW!" Pickle leaped up into the air, her fur standing on end like pins on a pincushion.

**CUSTOMER ANNOUNCEMENT:
THE LIGHTING DEPARTMENT IS CLOSED
UNTIL FURTHER NOTICE!**

At the sound of the tannoy, Pickle raced away across the beams, springing from one to the other. But as she jumped, her bandages got tangled round her back paws and she tripped. She grabbed hold of a nearby electrical cable in an attempt to break her fall and suddenly she found herself dangling in mid-air. She gripped the cable with her paws, but they were still slippery from the windscreen washer fluid and she began to slide downwards.

UNDEAD PETS

"Hold on, Pickle!" Joe said under his breath.

Pickle looked at him desperately. Then, without thinking, she bit down on the cable with her teeth.

"NO!" yelled Joe. He was no electrical expert, but even he didn't think biting a cable was a very good idea.

And he was right.

BANG!

For one ghastly second Pickle lit up like a light bulb.

Then all the lights went out.

Everyone gasped. The store manager's mouth opened like a goldfish and Toby breathed, "Wow!"

"'Joe!" Pickle yowled miserably from above, her teeth still clenched on the cable. "Help!"

Despite short-circuiting every light in the shop, Joe could see Pickle wasn't hurt – undead pets obviously couldn't feel pain.

"Jump!" he hissed.

"Who are you talking to, squirt?" Sarah glared at him.

"Er ... the squirrel," muttered Joe. "I saw it up there a minute ago."

"What squirrel?" The store manager peered down at him, his face like thunder. "Did you bring a squirrel into my shop?"

But before Joe could answer, the cable snapped and Pickle plummeted to the ground. And then Joe felt water sprinkling down.

"Why is it raining in here?" asked Toby.

Dad grimaced. "I think the shop's emergency sprinkler system has kicked in!"

Water was spraying down on them from above, as though someone had turned on a giant shower. There were shouts and yells, and customers ran for the doors. But it was too late. Everyone was already soaked.

CHAPTER THREE

"I still don't see how one small squirrel could cause so much trouble," said Mum.

Joe and his family were sitting round the kitchen table, having a late lunch. After the incident in the DIY store, they'd spent an hour in the manager's office, trying to convince him that Joe hadn't brought a squirrel into the shop. The manager didn't have any evidence, so he had eventually let them go.

"Maybe it wasn't a squirrel," said Sarah. "We only have freak-boy's word for it!"

UNDEAD PETS

"Hey!" shouted Joe.

"Don't call him that, Sarah," Mum said.

Joe scowled at his sister and tried to kick her under the table. But she quickly moved her legs out of the way.

"Well, it must have been an animal of some sort to make such a mess," said Dad.

Joe felt his cheeks redden. If only they knew! Luckily, Pickle had run out of the shop as soon as the sprinkler had started. But Joe knew it wouldn't be long before she appeared again. He glanced at the clock. "Can I go out now? I'm meeting some mates to play football."

Mum nodded.

"Can I come, too?" said Toby, stuffing the last of his salad in his cheeks like a hamster.

Joe made a face. Saturday afternoons were his favourite time of the week. He always spent them in the park playing football with his best mate, Matt, and some other kids from school. After

such a crazy morning, he was looking forward
to it even more than usual. He definitely didn't
want to have to look after his little brother all
afternoon.

"That would be nice," said Mum, ignoring
Joe's grumpy expression. "It'll give Dad a chance
to get on with the painting. And I can do some
weeding. The front garden is like a jungle!"

Joe groaned. "Can't Sarah look after Toby?"

"I've got a friend coming over," she said
smugly.

Toby looked at him pleadingly.

"OK, fine," Joe sighed.

Undead Pets

It was a sunny afternoon, and by the time they got to the park, it was full of people – dog walkers, joggers, families picnicking and loads of kids from school.

Matt was there already, kicking a ball with some other boys. He waved when he saw Joe and Toby. "Hey, Joe! It's your turn in goal this week!" Matt grinned and kicked the ball to Joe.

"Great!" Joe replied sarcastically. He hated being stuck in goal.

Joe dribbled the ball over towards the goal while Matt and the other kids made two teams. As the youngest, Toby was left to last, but eventually Joe's mate Ben took pity on him and let Toby join his team – playing against his big brother. Not that Joe cared. He had other worries. He'd just spotted who was in the other goal. Nicholas Branch. Or Nick the Stick as he

Undead Pets

was known, because he was so tall and thin. He was the best goalie in school, which meant Joe would have to try extra hard to keep his side from defeat.

Joe was blissfully lost in the game until suddenly he spotted something — a flash of grey disappearing into a clump of bushes.

It was Pickle.

"Great!" he muttered. "That's all I need."

UNDEAD PETS

Joe ignored her, hoping she'd go away again.

But after a few minutes, when all the action had moved to the other end of the pitch, she darted over to him, her loose bandages flapping in the breeze.

"Hi, Joe," she said, wrapping herself round his legs and butting his knees with her head. "Come with me! I need your help to protect my sister. I can show you the way to my house."

"Not now!" said Joe, trying to keep an eye on the ball. The players were heading back up the pitch, but Pickle didn't seem to have noticed.

"It won't take long," she whined.

"Later," said Joe, glaring at her. "Can't you see, I'm busy!"

As he spoke there was a sudden warning shout from Matt, and the ball whizzed over Joe's head, straight into the back of the net.

"Goal!" Toby cried proudly. He'd never scored against his big brother before.

The other boys on Toby's team cheered.

"Stop daydreaming, Joe!" yelled Matt.

Joe scowled, and kicked the ball as far down the field as he could. When the rest of the players had run off, he turned angrily to Pickle – but she'd vanished.

"Up here, Joe."

He glanced up. There was Pickle, clinging to the crossbar.

"That ball nearly hit me!" she moaned. "Please can we go now?"

"No!" Joe snapped. "Later!"

He tried to concentrate on the game, but it was hard with an undead cat above his head. He let another goal in, but then his team equalized. It didn't last long, because "the Bull" – Jake Bellingham – got the ball. Everyone called him the Bull because he bulldozed his way through the opposition! There was no stopping him now.

Joe gulped. The Bull was hurtling down the pitch towards him, dodging his team's defenders. Joe squatted, ready to make a dive for the ball, when suddenly a dog started barking nearby...

UNDEAD PETS

"A dog! Save me, Joe!" squealed Pickle. She dropped like a stone, right on to Joe's head, wrapping her bandaged tail round his face and blocking his view, just as the ball sailed past him into the net. GOAL!

Undead Pets

"What's with you today?" Matt asked as they walked home. "You missed four easy saves!"

Joe shrugged. "Er, a wasp was buzzing around my face."

Matt sighed. Toby, meanwhile, couldn't stop grinning. "Four—three! Four—three!" he sang, while Pickle scampered behind them, trying to keep up, her bandage trailing along the ground. Every so often she'd yowl, "Wait for me, Joe!"

But Joe ignored her. He'd had enough of being the Protector of Undead Pets. He needed to find a way of undoing the wish on the amulet.

"By the way," said Matt. "Can I come round to your house tomorrow? My aunt and uncle are visiting and I don't want to get stuck playing with my cousins!"

UNDEAD PETS

Joe grinned. He knew how much Matt hated having to entertain the twins, Lily and Lolly. "Sure," he said, glad to be back on good terms with his best mate. He just hoped he'd have got rid of Pickle by then.

Joe and Toby left Matt at the corner of their road and headed for home. Mum, who was doing some weeding in the front garden, called to them. "How did it go?"

UNDEAD PETS

"I scored a goal and beat Joe!" beamed Toby.

"Well done, Toby!" she smiled, then added, "Bad luck, though, Joe."

Joe made a grumpy face and continued to ignore Pickle, who was now rubbing her head against his legs, trying to get his attention.

"This'll cheer you up," said Mum, pulling a postcard out of the back pocket of her jeans and handing it to Joe. "It's from Uncle Charlie."

Joe felt a shiver of excitement. After trawling the internet and finding no information on how to reverse the wish he'd made on the Amulet of Anubis, he'd sent Uncle Charlie an email asking him for help with the undead pet problem. Maybe this was his reply! Maybe he knew a secret way of sending Pickle packing! Joe glanced at the picture on the front. It showed an old ruined city. Then he turned the card over and read the message.

HAVING A GREAT TIME
IN BOLIVIA - TIWANAKU
IS AMAZING! LOTS OF
STORIES TO TELL.
HOPE YOU'RE ENJOYING
YOUR PETS, JOE!
SEE YOU SOON.

LOVE, UNCLE CHARLIE x

JOE EDMUNDS
34 WOODSTOCK ROAD
LANCASTER
LANCS.
UNITED KINGDOM

And that was it. Not so much as a whisker of advice on how to get rid of the zombie animals who were haunting him.

"I don't know why he thinks you've got pets," said Mum, wiping her hands on her jeans. "He knows I'm allergic!" As if to prove the point, she wrinkled her nose and sneezed once, and then again, much louder.

Pickle froze, her eyes wide with terror at the noise.

UNDEAD PETS

"Have you been stroking dogs in the park?" Mum asked, rubbing her nose. "Something seems to be making me—"

And then she sneezed so loudly it was like a car had backfired!

It was too much for Pickle. She took off like a bullet, racing down the path and disappearing through Joe's front door.

Joe sighed. *Great! That's all I need,* he thought. *Another undead pet that sets off Mum's allergies!*

CHAPTER FOUR

"Pickle?" Joe whispered, peering into the dining room. "Are you in here?"

He'd already looked in the kitchen, the living room and the cupboard under the stairs.

"Pickle!" he hissed, feeling cross now. "I can't help you unless you stop hiding." It wasn't as though he wanted to find her, but he knew that the longer he took to solve the cat's problems, the longer she'd be bothering him.

Joe went upstairs to continue the search. He looked in all the bedrooms and the bathroom. He finally found her inside the airing

cupboard, curled up
in the laundry
basket.

"Has that
awful woman
gone?" said
Pickle miserably.

"That's my mum you're talking about!" said
Joe. "She can't help being allergic to you."

"I think *I'm* allergic to *her* — or at least to
the sound she makes when she sneezes." Pickle
buried her face in her paws. "I hate loud noises!"

Joe sighed. Why did undead pets have to be
so difficult?

Pickle looked up at him. "Do you know what
would make me feel better?"

Joe shrugged.

"A cuddle."

"*What?*"

Undead Pets

"You know, a stroke along my back and a tickle behind my ears. It always calms me down," said Pickle.

Joe grimaced. He really didn't want to touch her. Apart from smelling really bad, she was wrapped up in filthy bandages.

"Please, Joe," pleaded Pickle.

Joe took a deep breath and reluctantly reached out a hand to stroke her. He shuddered. She felt cold and damp, and the closer he got, the worse she smelled!

"That's nice," she purred. "And don't forget to tickle my ears."

Joe tried not to look at the dirty bandages wrapped around Pickle's head.

"Mmm, yes, that's lovely," purred Pickle as Joe rubbed her ears. "And just above my nose is nice, too."

It was going to be a long afternoon!

But just then Pickle stopped purring and looked anxious again. "You don't have a dog, do you?"

"No," said Joe. "I wish I did – I love dogs. Why?"

"I'm terrified of dogs! It was a horrible mean dog that caused my death."

Joe raised his eyebrows. "Really?" He didn't want to ask how, but he couldn't help himself. "So what happened?"

Pickle sighed. "I had a wonderful life. Everything was going so well..."

Me and my sister Pebbles lived happily with a girl called Maya...

Until her brother, Jay, got a pug puppy called Bonsai.

He wanted to play, but we didn't.

He chased me into the road. A car hit me!

SPLAT!

The vet tried to bandage me back together again, but it was too late...

Joe wasn't sure what to say. "Er ... sorry. Do you want me to re-tie your bandage for you, so you don't trip up again?"

Pickle nodded, and started to purr. "I just wish I was properly dead – that I could pass over peacefully. But I can't do that until I make sure the same thing doesn't happen to my sister Pebbles." She stared at Joe. "And that's why I need your help. I need you to go to my house and make sure Bonsai behaves better, so that Pebbles is safe."

Joe frowned. "But I don't know the first thing about puppy training. And anyway, I can't just walk into your old house and start telling your family how to sort out their dog!"

Pickle climbed on to Joe's knee. "But you must!" she said, butting his chin with her head. "Otherwise my sister might meet the same fate."

Joe tried not to breathe. He really didn't like being so close to Pickle. The smell was awful!

He wriggled to try and get her off his knee, but she dug her claws into his legs.

"Please, Joe, please help me!" she wailed.

"OK, OK!" Joe yelped. "Just stop spiking me! Maybe I could go over there tomorrow."

Pickle purred louder than ever. "I knew you'd find a way to fix things."

"Mmm," he said, grimacing as she curled up happily on his lap. He wasn't at all sure how he was going to solve this one!

CHAPTER FIVE

Joe was still trying to come up with a plan when Mum called him down to dinner a few hours later. Pickle had already made herself quite at home, nosing around his room.

"Stop that!" Joe reached down and retrieved his most treasured possession – a glass eye that had once belonged to a real pirate. Uncle Charlie had given it to him years ago. Normally it had pride of place on top of Joe's chest of drawers. But the minute Pickle saw it, she'd knocked it off the chest, and had been chasing it round the room ever since.

"Stay here – and stay out of trouble!" said Joe, replacing the eyeball on the chest before heading for the door.

"But who'll look after me?" wailed Pickle.

"You'll be just fine on your own." Joe raced downstairs before Pickle could start moaning again. "What's for dinner, Mum?" he asked as he walked into the kitchen.

"Spag bol," said Mum, who was draining the spaghetti at the sink. Thankfully, she seemed to have stopped sneezing for the moment. "Can you bring in another chair, Joe?" she added. "Sarah's got Gabriella staying for dinner."

Joe groaned. All Sarah's friends were as grotty as she was, but Gabriella was the worst. Thankfully they'd been up in Sarah's bedroom all afternoon, listening to music, so he hadn't had to see them! But that was about to change…

He heard the giggling before he saw them.

"Hi, Joe. How's the squirrel?" Gabriella smirked as she came into the kitchen with Sarah.

Joe glared at them both.

"Let's not talk about squirrels," said Dad. "I've had enough of them for one day!"

"How was football, Joe?" Sarah asked pointedly as she sat down and started eating her spaghetti. "Toby told me he scored a goal against you."

Toby grinned.

Joe was just about to say something mean to his sister when he felt a sharp stab in his leg. It was Pickle! She was clawing her way up on to his lap!

"Hey!" he yelped, as she dug her claws into his knee.

Everybody jumped at the sudden outburst.

"Are you all right, Joe?" asked Mum.

"I can't believe you left me on my own!" Pickle whined. "Anything could have happened."

Undead Pets

"I'm fine, thanks, Mum, just stiff from football." He glanced down at Pickle, who was getting comfy on his lap. "Sit still!" he hissed.

Sarah rolled her eyes. "He does that sometimes," she said to Gabriella. "Talks to his imaginary friends."

"Sarah!" said Mum sharply. "Leave Joe alone."

After that everyone ate in silence. Joe tried to enjoy his dinner, but Pickle was restless. She poked her nose up to take a look at everyone, then crawled on to the table.

Joe gasped. He still couldn't get used to the fact that he was the only one who could see the undead pets! He tried to act normal, but it wasn't easy with a phantom cat sitting next to his plate.

Pickle started cleaning herself. As she did, her bandaged tail dropped in Joe's dinner.

"Move!" Joe whispered.

"What?" said Pickle, her tail still on his plate.

UNDEAD PETS

"Don't do that!" hissed Joe.

"Don't do what?" snapped Sarah, rolling her eyes at her friend. "Who are you talking to, Joe?"

Gabriella giggled. "It's not the squirrel, is it? Has it popped in for a bit of spaghetti?"

The girls sniggered, but Joe was too busy watching Pickle, who had started licking her bandages. He grimaced. Suddenly he didn't feel hungry any more, and laid down his fork.

"Are you feeling OK, Joe?" Dad raised an eyebrow. "It's not like you to leave half your dinner."

"I'm just a bit full." Then he heard a sniff and Mum started rubbing her eyes.

"There's jam roly-poly for pudding," she said, getting up to fetch a tissue.

Sarah's eyes lit up. "My favourite!"

"I'll clear the plates," said Dad, stacking them up and taking them over to the sink.

Mum dished the jam roly-poly into the pudding bowls and handed them round.

Pickle, meanwhile, had stopped licking her bandages and was making strange heaving noises. Joe looked at her suspiciously. Just at that moment she coughed up a load of disgusting green hairballs all over the table. Some even landed in Joe's bowl.

"Urrrgh!" he gasped, poking the green sludge with his spoon.

"What is it? Doesn't it taste good?" asked Mum.

"Mine does!" snapped Sarah. "And if you're

not going to eat yours, I'll have it!"

Before Joe could reply, she swiped his bowl and started wolfing down the jam roly-poly. Of course, Sarah couldn't see Pickle – *or* the green hairballs she'd coughed up into Joe's bowl! But Joe could. He watched his sister slurping them down and grimaced.

YUCK!

Undead Pets

Mum, meanwhile, was rubbing her nose and sniffing a lot. Then, suddenly, she exploded into a series of loud sneezes!

"Heeelp!" Pickle leaped on to Joe's shoulder, yowling, "Save me, Joe! Make the noise stop!"

"I don't feel well," said Joe, standing up, with Pickle still clinging on to his shoulder like a crazy parrot. "I think I'll go and lie down."

"Hey!" yelled Sarah. "It's your turn to do the dishes!"

"I'll do double tomorrow," he promised, then fled.

"That awful noise!" wailed Pickle, still clinging to Joe's shoulder as he ran up the stairs.

"Stop making such a fuss! It's me that should be moaning – thanks to your disgusting table manners I didn't get to finish my dinner. I'm starving!"

Pickle turned her head away in a huff. She leaped off Joe's shoulder as soon as they reached his room. "It's not my fault," she moaned. "Your house is just too noisy!"

"Well, why don't you go somewhere else?"

Pickle glared at him for a moment, then turned her back.

Joe ignored her for the rest of the evening. Pickle, who was still in a sulk, curled up on Joe's bed and went to sleep, while Joe played computer games.

Pickle was still asleep as Joe got into his pyjamas. She didn't stir as he pulled back the duvet. And even when he tried to get into bed, she didn't move.

"Hey! Wake up and stop hogging the bed!" Joe said sternly, pushing Pickle off his pillow.

Pickle's tail drooped and she crawled to the furthest corner of the bed. But as soon as Joe turned the light off, she crept under the covers and curled up in the hollow between Joe's chest and the duvet.

"Get lost, Pickle!" Joe turned away and lay on his other side, but the cat didn't care. She crept back up, nuzzling his cheek and squeezing herself in to the space between his shoulder and head.

"Cut it out!" Joe moaned, shoving Pickle away. The smell was unbearable. "Go and find your own bed!"

He rolled over and began to get comfy. But just as he was drifting off, she was back again.

And then the purring started.

Joe groaned. It was like lying next to a steam train – a stinky steam train!

"Be quiet!" He stuck his fingers in his ears, but he could still hear it.

After a while, Joe was too tired to even tell her off any more. He stuffed his head under his pillow and eventually fell asleep.

CHAPTER SIX

But Joe didn't sleep for long. Whenever he dropped off, Pickle would stretch out and wake him up. Or worse still, she'd snuggle up really close with her stinky bandages right next to his nose! Then Pickle decided it was playtime. She raced round the room, climbed his curtains and knocked down his glass eye, bashing it against the skirting board. She made such a racket that Sarah came and banged on his door, telling him to shut up!

When Joe woke up the next morning he was

UNDEAD PETS

lying on the edge of the bed with one leg dangling out. Pickle was curled up luxuriously in the middle.

"Morning, Joe," the cat yawned as she woke. "Sleep well?"

"No!" he growled. "Thanks to *you*!" He had to get rid of her – and fast!

UNDEAD PETS

After a quick bite of breakfast, Joe decided he'd have to go and find Maya. All Joe had to do now was come up with a good excuse to get out of the house. As soon as he saw Dad dressed in his scruffiest old clothes, ready to finish painting Sarah's room, Joe knew just what to do.

"Dad, how about I fetch the paper today, so you can get on with the decorating?"

Dad eyed Joe suspiciously. He wasn't usually so helpful first thing on a Sunday morning. "OK. Take some money out of my wallet. And don't blow it on sweets!"

Joe grabbed the money and made for the door, before his dad could tell him to take Toby! "Come on!" he called to Pickle, who was already outside waiting impatiently on the wall. "Show me the way to your house."

UNDEAD PETS

"Are you sure this is the right way?" puffed Joe as he followed Pickle down yet another overgrown path, behind some old garages a few streets away. She flicked her tail and didn't reply. This was the way she always went home – the cat's way. She was taking him on a direct route through gardens, around bins, behind sheds and over fences. It wasn't her fault that Joe only had two legs, and couldn't keep up!

Undead Pets

As Joe clambered over yet another fence, Pickle suddenly took off, veering left, then right, then disappearing into an old bit of piping that was poking out of the ground.

"Hey! Where are you going?" yelled Joe.

Two minutes later, Pickle reappeared, covered in dirt and cobwebs. "Sorry," she said. "I got the scent of a mouse."

And then, in a flash, she was off again.

Undead Pets

By the time they got to Maya's house, Joe was exhausted. His jeans were filthy from scrambling over fences and he had several splinters in his hands. As they approached the house, he could hear the sound of yapping.

"Bonsai!" yowled Pickle. She made a leap for Joe, clawing her way up his body until she was on his shoulder.

"Hey!" Joe yelped, as Pickle disappeared into his hood, trembling with fear. "Get off!" But she clung on, wrapping her front paws round his neck, her claws digging into his flesh.

"Ow! Watch it with those claws, Pickle!"

"Save me from that terrifying dog!" she yowled.

"What have you got to worry about? You're already dead!" said Joe, through gritted teeth. But Pickle just dug her claws in deeper.

Just then he heard a loud meow from the garden.

UNDEAD PETS

"Pebbles!" wailed Pickle. "We've got to help her!"

As Joe got closer, he could see a little grey cat with white paws sitting halfway up a tree. And at the bottom, yapping, jumping and wriggling around, was Bonsai.

The puppy was small and stocky, with short legs and a squashed-looking face.

Pickle hid her face in Joe's hood. "Make him stop! Make him stop!"

But before Joe could do anything, the front door opened and a girl came running out.

"Maya!" yowled Pickle.

The girl tied to shoo the pup away from the tree. But he seemed to think it was a game, and bounded around her feet excitedly. "Leave her alone, Bonsai!" she yelled, sounding close to tears.

"Do something, Joe!" Pickle howled.

Joe spotted a ball lying in the shrubbery and leaned over the wall to grab it.

"Hey, Bonsai! Good dog, over here!"

"What are you doing?" shrieked Pickle, shaking like crazy inside his hood. "Don't call him over to me!"

But Joe ignored her. He bounced the ball a few times on the ground, then shouted to the pup, "Come on, boy, over here!"

UNDEAD PETS

Bonsai came running, his little pink tongue sticking out, his tiny curly tail wagging. Joe threw the ball over to the other side of the garden and Bonsai bounded after it, yapping excitedly.

It was just the distraction Maya needed. While the pup chased the ball, she climbed the lower branches of the tree, grabbed Pebbles and took her swiftly inside the house.

UNDEAD PETS

Moments later, Maya was back.

"Thanks very much," she said, smiling at Joe.

"No worries. I'm Joe, by the way." He picked up the ball that the puppy had brought him, and threw it again.

"I'm Maya," she replied as Bonsai took off across the garden like a rocket.

"He's full of beans," grinned Joe.

"Yeah, he is," said Maya with a sigh. "He's cute, but he plays rough. My cat doesn't like it."

Pickle was leaning out of Joe's hood now, peering round his neck like a meerkat. "Ask her about me!" she said. "Come on!"

"So, what's your cat called?" Joe swatted Pickle away.

"Pebbles," said Maya. "She used to have a sister called Pickle, but she died, and it was all Bonsai's fault!" She glared at the pup. "He chased Pickle out into the road, and she was hit by a car."

"Exactly!" said Pickle crossly. "Bad dog!"

Bonsai was lying in the grass, rolling on his back.

"Er ... that's a shame," said Joe, bending down to tickle Bonsai's tummy. Pickle, who was still huddled in his hood, hissed at the puppy. "I'm sure he doesn't mean to be naughty. Maybe he just thinks everyone wants to play."

Maya nodded. "I suppose so. I just wish he'd leave Pebbles alone. I don't want the same thing to happen to her."

Just then there was a shout from inside the house. "Maya – phone!"

"I've got to go," she said. "Thanks again for your help."

Joe nodded. Then she was gone.

Joe threw the ball for the puppy, then

walked back out on to the street. He needed to get back before his parents started to wonder where he'd got to.

But Pickle had other ideas. She jumped down on to the pavement and darted round in front of Joe, blocking his path. "Where are you going?" she said. "You haven't saved Pebbles from that bully yet."

"I'm not sure there's anything I can do, Pickle," said Joe, stepping over her.

"What?" The cat thrashed her tail from side to side. "But you have to do something!"

"Pebbles just has to learn to stand up to him."

"What?" Pickle howled. "How is she supposed to do that?"

Joe shrugged. The truth was, he had no idea.

CHAPTER SEVEN

"Maybe you could just go back and haunt Bonsai?" suggested Joe as they headed to the newsagent's. They were going by the main road this time, rather than by Pickle's route. "Every time he bothers Pebbles, you could just clobber him with a tin of paint or smash a glass chandelier or something!"

"That was an accident," Pickle said. "And anyway, I don't like dogs. And I don't like noise. I just want to rest in peace."

Joe sighed. "What we really need is a tough

cat who can teach Bonsai a lesson."

"What? How?"

"Well, that's how Dad always tells me to deal with bullies. You know, stand up to them. Not that Bonsai's a bully, really — he's just young and playful. He doesn't know any better. But a really tough cat could teach him a bit of cat respect."

Pickle cocked her head to one side. "I know a cat like that," she said. "Fang! He lives behind the bins at the back of the fish and chip shop."

"An alley cat?"

Pickle nodded. "I met him one night when I was out exploring. We had a disagreement over a piece of fish. He thought it belonged to him," said Pickle crossly. "But I found it first!"

Joe grinned. "Did you have a fight?"

"Certainly not! I … well, I ran away, actually."

That sounded about right, thought Joe. Pickle wasn't much of a fighter.

"I bet Fang could teach that cheeky pup some manners," said Pickle.

"But even if he could, how would we get him here? It's not as though I can just catnap him!"

"Why not?" Pickle said impatiently. "And, anyway, you wouldn't need to catnap him. Stray cats will do anything for food and Fang has a huge appetite! You could just leave a trail of food from the bins back to Bonsai."

Joe raised his eyebrows. "Like Hansel and Gretel and the trail of breadcrumbs? That's ridiculous!"

But Pickle wouldn't stop going on about Fang, and by the time they got to the shop, Joe had agreed to have a quick look down the alley beside the fish and chip shop.

UNDEAD PETS

"I'm going to get Dad's newspaper first," said Joe.

Inside the newsagent, he spotted a shelf of pet food. At the far end were a few bags of cat treats. Joe sighed. He'd probably need some of those if he was going in search of an alley cat!

"I was supposed to be using my pocket money to buy Mum a new sponge," he grumbled as he picked up three bags and took them to the till along with Dad's newspaper.

Luckily for Joe, the fish and chip shop was closed on Sunday mornings, so he was able to sneak down the side without anyone noticing. There were four black wheelie bins, jammed full of rotting rubbish from the takeaway.

Joe didn't want to get too close.

"Maybe Fang's not here," he said, hopefully.

"Look properly," yowled Pickle. "He's probably round the back."

"Urgh!" groaned Joe. "It stinks!"

UNDEAD PETS

The bins were overflowing with old cartons and tins, potato peelings, fish heads and greasy paper. Next to the bins were bottles stacked up in crates, surrounded by wasps and flies. Joe grimaced as fish bones crunched under his feet. "This place is foul!"

"I can't smell a thing," said Pickle.

That was probably because her own breath smelled so bad, Joe thought, but he didn't say anything.

The GODFATHER

The CODFATHER

"I can't see Fang," said Joe, having a quick look behind the bins. But just then he heard a deep throaty growl from nearby.

"Under there!" hissed Pickle, running to hide behind Joe.

He got down on his hands and knees amongst the rubbish and peered underneath the bins. The stench was awful! At first he couldn't see anything, but as he got used to the darkness, he spotted a pair of big green eyes glaring back at him. Fang?

"Here, puss..." said Joe, throwing a few cat treats towards the creature.

It gobbled them up like a vacuum cleaner, then growled for more.

"Come and get them, then," said Joe, holding out a few treats in his hand. Maybe this idea wasn't so bonkers after all! "Out you come."

But just then, a familiar voice made Joe jump.

UNDEAD PETS

"What are you doing under there, Joe?"

He looked up.

It was Matt and his dad, carrying a newspaper, some bread rolls and a carton of milk.

"Urgh!" Matt wrinkled his nose. "It stinks round here!"

Joe grinned sheepishly. "Er ... well..."

"I knew it was you," said Matt. "I spotted you sneaking down here when we went in for the papers. Since when did you start rummaging in bins?"

Joe stood up and wiped a few fish bones off his knees. "You see..." he floundered, desperately trying to think of a good fib. "I, well..."

But just then a growling Fang suddenly shot out from under the bin!

CHAPTER EIGHT

Fang was probably the most gruesome-looking cat Joe had ever seen. He was a massive old ginger tom. A chunk was missing out of one ear and he had several battle scars on his face. His tail looked like it had been put through a mincing machine and the stump that remained was horribly chewed. But the scariest thing about him was the big pointy tooth that poked out of one side of his mouth, making him look like a piranha. Joe could see why Pickle hadn't wanted to argue with him!

Fang stalked towards Joe, and Pickle immediately panicked. She raced up Joe's leg and disappeared inside his hood again. Joe threw a handful of treats at Fang.

"I'm not sure it's a good idea to feed stray cats, Joe," said Matt's dad.

"Ah well, you see, he's not a stray," stuttered Joe. "I think he's my friend Maya's lost cat."

"Maya?" Matt looked puzzled. "Who's she?"

"Er, she's..." said Joe, thinking quickly. "Her dad works with my dad," he fibbed. "We've known each other since we were little, but I don't see her much."

78

Matt grinned. "She's not your secret girlfriend, is she?"

Joe's face went red. "No! Of course not. It's just ... er ... my dad told me she'd lost her cat, and when I was going into the newsagent's, I thought I spotted it running down here, so I thought I'd take a look. Yup, that's definitely her cat," he said, looking at Fang, who was growling for more treats, his stumpy tail whipping back and forth impatiently.

"There you go, er, Pickle," said Joe, scattering a few more treats on the ground.

"Pickle?" Matt's dad chuckled. "He doesn't look much like a 'Pickle' to me – 'Killer', maybe, or 'Bruiser', perhaps, but definitely not 'Pickle'. That's a bit of a weedy name for such a monster!"

"What a cheek!" whined the real Pickle.

"Oh, he's actually a real softy," said Joe, gingerly reaching his hand out to stroke Fang's head, willing the cat not to bite him. "Actually,

UNDEAD PETS

I'm going to take him home to Maya now," Joe said, scratching Fang behind the ear. Thankfully, he seemed to have taken a bit of a shine to Joe — most likely because of the treats — and so Joe scooped him up into his arms. He tried not to grimace. Fang was big and dirty and ponged almost as badly as Pickle.

UNDEAD PETS

Suddenly Matt had an idea. "Can we give Joe a lift to his friend's house?" he asked his dad. "I mean, look at him — that cat weighs a ton!"

"No!" squealed Pickle, peeping out of Joe's hood. "I hate cars!"

But it was true. Joe was already struggling to carry Fang. He was an enormous animal and weighed twice as much as a normal cat.

Matt's dad shrugged. "I suppose so, but you'll have to call your mum first, Joe, and check it's OK." He handed Joe his mobile.

"Dad," Matt said. "Would it be all right for me to tag along with Joe?"

"What?" Joe gulped. A lift to Maya's house was one thing, but he wasn't so sure about having Matt with him. How would he get away with all his fibs!

"You see, Joe invited me round to his house later today, so it would probably be easier if I just went with him now."

UNDEAD PETS

Joe had totally forgotten. He had said Matt could come round to his house to escape his young cousins. He looked at his friend's desperate face and nodded. "That's right, Mr Adams. I did invite Matt round today."

Matt's dad shrugged. "OK, fine, but call your mum first, Joe."

He dialled home and his mum answered. "Hi, Mum," he said. He wasn't very good at telling fibs. "Er ... I'm down at the newsagent's and I've spotted my friend Maya's cat — you know, the one who's been missing for weeks..." He didn't give her the chance to ask "Who's Maya?" or "What cat?"

"Well, anyway, Matt and his dad are here, and they've offered to give me a lift to Maya's house to drop her cat off, if that's OK with you."

Luckily, Mum sounded like she was in the middle of something. He could hear Sarah moaning in the background about the new paint on her bedroom walls being the wrong shade of purple. Mum was keen to get off the phone, and quickly agreed to the plan. They all got in to the car and set off, with Joe giving directions from the back seat.

Fang, however, was not an easy-going passenger. He didn't like the car at all, and no number of treats would make him sit still. Pickle hated the car, too, and spent the entire journey sitting in Joe's hood, yowling miserably.

"Cut it out!" whispered Joe. But Pickle just howled louder – the car was bringing back bad memories of her accident.

"He's driving too fast!" she wailed. "It was a fast car that killed me! What if it happens again?"

"Don't be ridiculous!" whispered Joe.

Meanwhile, Fang had had enough of the car, too. He was on the move.

UNDEAD PETS

"Hey!" yelled Matt's dad as the alley cat clambered along the parcel shelf. "He's blocking my view!"

Joe reached out to grab him, but Fang gave a grumpy growl and bared his teeth – they were big, yellow and very sharp-looking!

"Are you sure that's your friend's cat?" asked Matt as Fang dived on to the floor by Joe's feet and sat there glowering up at them. "He doesn't look ... well ... very friendly."

"Yeah, er, I'm sure it's him. At least, I think so," Joe shrugged, scratching the back of his neck. It was probably Pickle's fur tickling him. Either that or she'd given him fleas – nasty zombie fleas, probably! Or maybe Fang had fleas?

Eventually they turned into Maya's street, just as Fang started attacking the upholstery in a desperate bid to claw his way out of the car.

"Which house is it, Joe?" asked Matt's dad, anxiously watching Fang in his rear-view mirror.

"That one," said Joe. "The one with the big tree."

As soon as the car stopped, Joe opened his door with one hand and tried to grab Fang with the other. But the cat was far too quick – he shot past Joe and jumped up on to Maya's garden wall, where he sat glaring at Joe. Fang had obviously decided that he and Joe weren't friends after all.

Matt climbed out, too.

"See you later!" his dad shouted through the open car window as he drove off.

"Come on, Joe!" Pickle said impatiently. "What if Fang runs off? Go and ring the doorbell!"

But there was no need, because at that moment Pebbles came racing out of the cat flap, closely followed by Bonsai, who was panting and yapping wildly. He chased her across the garden, nipping at her heels.

"He's going to catch her!" wailed Pickle, gripping Joe's neck with her claws.

Moments later, the front door crashed open and Maya appeared, along with her little brother. They were arguing loudly.

"Get your dog away from my cat!" Maya was shouting.

"He just wants to play!" her brother yelled.

"Well, Pebbles doesn't *want* to play with him!"

Meanwhile, Bonsai carried on chasing the terrified cat through the shrubbery, across the lawn and in and out of the bushes.

"Do something, Joe!" squealed Pickle.

CHAPTER NINE

Without thinking, Joe flung the rest of the cat treats over the wall, then gave Fang a shove in the same direction. He did it quite gently, but all the same, the alley cat was not amused.

"MEOW!" he growled, landing with a thud on the lawn.

"Over here, Bonsai!" yelled Joe, but the little dog had already spotted Fang and was hurtling towards the new cat as fast as his short legs would carry him.

Fang did not look impressed by Bonsai.

UNDEAD PETS

Not one bit. He arched his back and hissed at the pup. Bonsai, however, was too young to spot the warning signs and continued charging towards the alley cat, panting and yapping, ready for a new game of chase. But unlike Pebbles, Fang didn't budge. He didn't run away. He stood his ground, his eyes glaring, his fur standing on end. His tail thrashed and he growled like a bear. Then Fang sprang at the puppy, his big tooth flashing in the sunlight raised his paw and swiped Bonsai across the nose!

UNDEAD PETS

Bonsai stopped and stared. For a second he didn't seem to know what had happened. Then he gave a loud whimper and scuttled back to hide behind Maya's little brother, Jay.

"He did it!" shrieked Pickle, jumping out of Joe's hood on to the wall and purring for all she was worth. "He's taught Bonsai a lesson!"

Just then, Maya spotted Joe and ran over. "You came back," she said.

Joe blushed and Matt gave him a look.

"Did you see what just happened?" beamed Maya. "That big stray cat just cuffed Bonsai!"

"Er ... yeah," said Joe nervously, trying not to look at Matt.

"Stray cat?" asked Matt in a puzzled voice. "Isn't he your cat, then?"

Maya laughed. "Of course not! That's my cat." She pointed to Pebbles, who was trotting cautiously over to Maya, still looking over her shoulder, as though she was expecting Bonsai to pounce on her at any moment.

"But Joe said *that* was your cat." Matt pointed to Fang, who had finished the cat treats and was now licking himself. "Joe found him over at the chip shop. He said you'd lost him."

"What?" Maya frowned. "My cat isn't lost!"

They both looked at Joe.

Pickle gave a chuckle. "Oops! Someone's in trouble now!"

Joe grinned awkwardly at Maya and Matt. "Well," he said, his palms feeling a bit sweaty. "I ... I thought you said you'd lost your cat – Pickle, wasn't it?"

At the sound of her name, Pickle yowled.

Maya looked shocked. "What? You thought that old ginger cat was Pickle? But I told you, Pickle is dead."

As she said the word, Pickle gave a sad sigh, and muttered. "I wish I was dead. Properly, I mean."

UNDEAD PETS

Joe was blushing bright red. Trying to wriggle out of fibs was seriously tricky! "Oh, sorry," he said, looking at the ground, "I must have heard you wrong." He glanced over Maya's shoulder, desperately searching for something to divert the attention from him. "Hey, look," he said. "Pebbles actually seems to like that ginger cat!"

UNDEAD PETS

Pebbles and Fang were nose to nose. But not in a we-hate-each-other sort of a way. They were sniffing each other and purring.

Pickle shrugged. "She's probably been a bit lonely without me."

Maya bent down to give Fang and Pebbles a stroke. "Well, I'm glad you got a bit muddled, Joe. It was good to see a cat standing up to Bonsai for a change."

"Yeah, but Bonsai is only little." said Joe. "I don't think he really want to hurt Pebbles, just play with her."

"Humph!" Pickle turned her back on Joe. "Look what happened when he played with *me*!"

Maya nodded. "Mum says that, too. She's booked him in for puppy training, so that might help. And now he knows cats have claws, maybe he won't be so rough!"

Joe looked over. The pup had stopped whimpering and was standing staring at them from the other end of the garden, next to Jay.

"Can me and Matt stay and play with Bonsai for a bit?"

Maya smiled. "Sure. That would be great." She turned to her brother. "Hey, Jay, bring Bonsai over here."

The pup was reluctant. He definitely didn't like walking past Fang, who was now sitting on the wall with Pebbles (and Pickle, though no one but Joe could see her!).

"Hello," said Jay shyly.

"You've got a great dog," said Joe, picking up Bonsai's ball. "Come on, boy – fetch!" He threw the ball across the lawn.

Bonsai hesitated for a millisecond, but he couldn't help himself – he had to chase it!

CHAPTER TEN

Joe and Matt carried on playing with the pup for a bit, while the cats watched from the wall. Joe had just thrown the ball when he glanced at Pickle and realized she was trying to get his attention. He ran over.

"Everything OK?" he whispered, pretending to stroke Pebbles.

"I think things are better now, Joe," Pickle said, purring softly. "Pebbles doesn't seem anxious any more, and Bonsai seems to have learned his lesson. I think it's time I was going."

Joe could see she was already beginning to fade.

"Thanks for everything, Joe. I'll never forget you."

Then Pickle disappeared completely, just as Maya's mum stuck her head out of the back door and called Maya and Jay into the house for lunch.

"You can come over again, if you like, Joe," Maya said. Joe blushed and Matt nudged his friend.

"Maybe," Joe mumbled, trying not to look at Matt, who was now making lovey-dovey faces.

As Pebbles followed Maya into the house, Joe noticed that Bonsai kept his distance. Hopefully he had learned some cat respect now. Joe wondered if it would last — he didn't fancy another visit from Pickle!

"What about him?" Matt nodded to Fang, who was still sitting on the wall.

Joe shrugged. "I should probably take him back to the chip shop, I suppose."

But just then Maya reappeared with a bowl of cat food. "Mum says I can give him some food." She stroked his mangled ears as she watched him tuck in. "He's a funny old thing. I wonder what his name is?"

"Er … something tough, I reckon," said Joe. "Like Fang, maybe."

Maya giggled. "Yeah, that suits him."

UNDEAD PETS

"Do you think they'll keep him?" Matt asked as he and Joe walked down the road, heading for home.

Joe shrugged. "Hope so. He'd definitely keep Bonsai in line, if they did."

Just then a raindrop landed on Joe's face. He glanced up at the sky. They'd been so busy playing with the puppy, neither of them had noticed the dark clouds above.

Matt zipped up his coat and Joe reached back to pull on his hood. As he did, he felt something wet and soggy in there.

It was a hairball – a green, sludgy reminder of Pickle.

Undead Pets

Joe shuddered. He definitely wouldn't miss those. Then he smiled. He was glad she'd passed over peacefully. And he was looking forward to having some peace and quiet of his own now.

"Joe, have you stepped in something?"

"What?"

Matt was sniffing the air. "Something smells really bad."

Joe checked his shoes. "It's not me."

Matt checked his. "Or me!"

Joe sniffed the air. He could smell it now, too – something horrible, like damp, sweaty socks, or stinky shoes. Joe heard a faint howling sound – in the distance, as though a dog was trying to call its owner. For a second, Joe wondered if it was Bonsai. He listened again. It was closer this time, and it definitely didn't sound like a puppy. It sounded like something bigger, much bigger...

UNDEAD PETS

What if it was another undead pet, come to offload all its worries on to him? There was only one thing for it...

"Come on!" he suddenly shouted to Matt. "Race you home!" And Joe took off down the street, running as fast as he could.

OUT NOW!

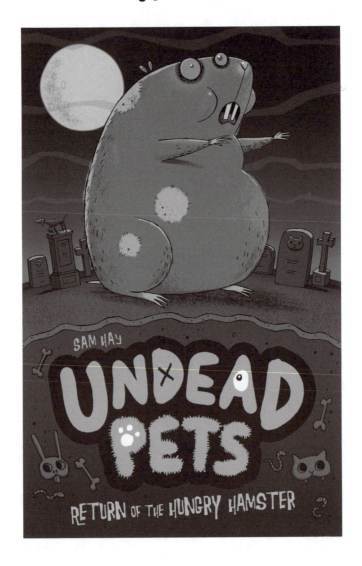

Joe is just an ordinary boy until he makes a wish on a spooky Egyptian amulet...

Now he's the Protector of UNDEAD PETS ... and there's a ravenous rodent on the rampage!

Dumpling the hamster got sucked up a vacuum cleaner. Can Joe help him sort out his unfinished business, so he can finally bite the dust?

OUT NOW!

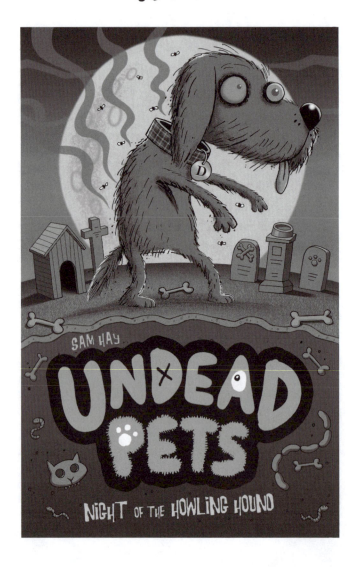

SAM HAY

UNDEAD PETS

NIGHT OF THE HOWLING HOUND

Joe is just an ordinary boy until he makes a wish on a spooky Egyptian amulet...

Now he's the Protector of UNDEAD PETS ... and there's a demented dog off the leash!

Dexter chased a squirrel right off the edge of a cliff. Can Joe help him give up the ghost once and for all?

OUT NOW!

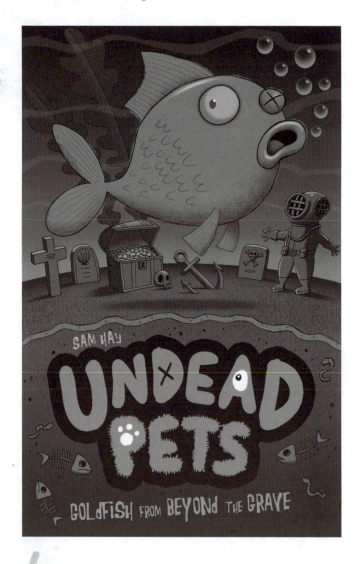

Joe is just an ordinary boy
until he makes a wish on a
spooky Egyptian amulet...

Now he's the Protector of
UNDEAD PETS ... and there's a
ghoulish goldfish making a splash!

Fizz the goldfish got flushed.
Can Joe help him take revenge so
he can go belly up forever?